How Buffalo-Stands-Firm Got His Name

His Name

A Black-Indian Boy's story:

An Adventure By Shay Jones

Robert Scott Temple- Cover Artist

Bill McCormick - Cover Design / Book Format

Stephan Platzer - Website Design

Maggie Geoteau - Editor

First I'd like to thank God/The Great Good Spirit for giving me the task of creating this adventure.

This story has come about from reading William Loren Katz's book Black Indians: Hidden Heritage and an exhaustive search for over 20 years about native nomads.

I am certain that there are many inaccuracies in my tale but I wished to tell a story of love and friendship.

Thanks to all who have given me advice. My spiritual prayer warriors: Alice Marie Williams, Pat cross, my niece Shawn Osborne, The Woods family, The Osborne Family, Richard R. Lefrak (passed on), Valerie Roebke, Denyse Leventman, E.W. and Monica Whittington, Vickie Markusic, Babbe Irving, Don Stark for the cover, The Ladies of Panama, Paragon Studios, and if I've forgotten anyone I apologize.

Much Love

Shay Jones

How Buffalo-Stands-Firm Got His Name
A Black-Indian Boy's story
By Shay Jones

Prologue

Three hundred years after the first intrusion of
European explorers, an onslaught of foreigners
sailed to the New World and was staking claims to
lands that had already been inhabited by various
ancient Indigenous Nomads who roamed the
continent for around 13,500 years. From across
Northern Asia, via a land bridge known as Beringia.

These early Paleo-Indian nomads spread throughout
the Americas, diversifying into many hundreds of
culturally distinct nations and tribes. They had their
own customs and their own names. "The True
Ones,The People,The Only Ones," and "Human
Beings" were some of their chosen names. They
were by their nature: teachers and caretakers of the
lands in which they lived, gathered, planted and
hunted. They moved seasonally with the animals
they shared their lives with which had always been
dependent on the land and the animals. They relied
on and identified with the Great Good Spirit, the
spirits of the animals that fed them and significantly
with that of the Buffalo. Nothing was wasted. And
the land was respected.

The new settlers saw the new world as a panoramic
marvel of breath-taking beauty that was free for the

taking. It was lush and unspoiled. It was a place to breathe clean air—for families to start new lives and businesses to start new economies. In time and with governmental agency help; many tribes/nations were forced into deadly altercations not of their own making. Natives were summarily threatened and driven from their sacred lands. And as a result of the decisions made by the "Great Fathers" in Washington; every nation lost. Chiefs were summoned to appear beforethe "Great Fathers" in Washington to sign land secession papers or else. These agreements would violently split each of the five tribal nations.

While throngs of people continued to pour into America for the massive land grab. And because of the rising population; more than a quarter million enslaved Africans were being brought by slave traders to work the burgeoning plantations in the southern colonies. In actuality, more people came to the "New World" in chains than all those who immigrated of their own free will. Black skinned people were dehumanized and were owned, traded and sold into slavery like livestock.

Heartbroken slaves would commit suicide. And those who managed to escape their unnatural captivity were more than eager to join with any nomadic bands that would take them in. As time would dictate, few tribes even allowed slaves to take mates and have children and in some cases would become blood brothers with them. Some even owned slaves and in rare circumstances people of African ancestry became chiefs to native clans but not without great sacrifice.

This is a fictional story of Kah-La Longbow, a ten year old boy whose Mulatto father escaped from slavery and mated with an Indian woman. In this tale, he gets his new name and starts his life as a young warrior; eventually becoming leader of his clan. As intended, no particular names of Indian tribes or Indians are given. This is a story of different cultures—how they struggled, survived and found love, even under constant threat.

Stranded: Kah-La and Yawns a Lot

In the cold Northern Plains in the winter following
the great "White Men's war", two young native
males, Kah-La and Yawns-a-Lot, sat hidden in the
blustery snowdrifts along an almost-frozen-over
creek. The two now found themselves stranded and
alone after a great earthquake struck their hunting
party a few days before. The boys were waiting in
desperation for the last few geese to land and feed on
their way south. Wrapped in their buffalo skin robes;
and grass lined mittens, the boys huddled together
for warmth, shivering in the piercing cold. The two
boys had managed to haphazardly put up a makeshift
tipi to harbor them while they hunted what little
game they could find.

The sky threatened—an approaching storm loomed
over the pristine landscape. It was white and silent—
deadly silent; except for the high pitch of the
screaming wind. Dead branches stuck out of the
nearby creek like falcons' claws. The boy's watched
the skies; anticipating the flocks of geese that would
fly overhead; on their way south. The two boys were
not unaccustomed to the winters. Except now they
were alone with fewer supplies.

Ten-year-old Kah-La was primed. His arm flexibly
rigid; his bow and arrow perched to strike at
anything that might become their next meal. The few
geese that landed; quickly flew off—not getting
close enough to kill; And slowly being drained by

battling the brutal cold with empty stomachs. They hadn't eaten in days. They were forced to conserve what rations they had left. And to stay alert and keep themselves from freezing, they continuously rubbed their hands and bodies to keep their circulation going and ward off frostbite. The winter's dilemma was upon them. There was little doubt of Coyote's interference. He was masterfully plunging them further into despair. (Coyote; often mischievous; a folk-tale character common with many Native First cultures). Legends vary.

The Destruction of a People

The mostly European settlers and their families were steadily changing the landscape; snatching it up acre by acre. Cutting down trees and turning the terrain into a wasteland. The government championed the settlers by destroying the lives of the people who had already been living on the lands. They cleared the lands, instead of following the herds. And with the building of new forts, towns and roads, Buffalo herds were no longer tens of millions strong across the plains, due to the ruthless endeavors ofmany unsavory characters that saw their way to greed. Deer, elk, and bison were also no longer as plentiful as they had once been. Supplies in the camps were scant because of the constant raiding and fighting, crops could not be planted and harvested.They became dependent on trading and bartering with whoever they'd safely come across. Relentless fighting was hard on weapons and clothing, putting further strain on all tribes. Bounties were put on the heads of many of the chiefs who resisted forced resettlement.

The armies of the long knives often waited till harvest time to up root the "Human Beings". They would waste no time packing their few belongings swiftly but the frailest of them would perish from their hardship. So in order to avoid contact with their enemies, the people were continuously on the move. Winters were dismal. While the men hunted for food, women warriors were left in charge to protect and defend the temporary camps. Tribal numbers continued to plummet. And it became virtually impossible for "The people" to travel long side the herds. "The People" were vastly outnumbered by settlers and military soldiers, their best and only defense was surprise and stealth as they counted coup when they raided and destroyed settlers' farms, rounding up livestock, kidnapping women and children and taking whatever grain, tools and supplies they could carry, then setting fire to the buildings and crops.Settlers were outraged.

And because of the raids, the existing government recruited more armies of long knives to drive "The Human Beings" away from the lands that they had taken. This led to more and more outposts and farms being destroyed and people killed. Back and forth, the bloody warfare went on and on.

With the continual arrival of the Europeans they would bring with them previously unknown diseases such as tuberculosis, influenza, cholera, typhoid fever and smallpox. Over time the disease of alcoholism would inflict the delicate "Human Being" population; and entire communities would be utterly affected and destroyed.

The Devastation of War

War and disease left wives without husbands, children without fathers and communities without warriors and chiefs. Only handfuls of warriors were left of many of the tribes. "The People" were starving to death. Small bands would somehow make their way to another clan's campfire and merge together for safety and survival. Winters were severe and uncompromising.

Women, children and elders would remain in temporary encampments while hunters, hunted. They shared whatever food they could find. Everyone was responsible to forage for firewood, roots and whatever food-source they could scavenge to keep one constant pot of stew going and the community alive. Remaining warriors would venture out; three and four braves at a time to scout, to hunt and keep one step ahead of the Long-knife soldiers and armed settlers, and other treacherous tribesmen who were being compensated to hunt capture or murder; if there was a bounty.

As young children Kah-La and Yawns-a-Lot often heard the complaints from the elders:

"Our great freedoms are over. Our way of life is no more.How can we send these people back to where they came from? We do not want them on our lands.They cannot be trusted.The white-man speaks with a forked tongue," was the rallying cry to all "Human Beings" communities.

And it was weeks earlier, when a hunting party from their community had gone to hunt and trap and had ended up being ambushed by armed militia men and scouts. In a hail of bullets, the small hunting party had to flee their former winter hunting grounds. Kah-La's father, Marcus, who was given the name; Buffalo's Heart Long Bow, had been shot in the back and was lying in his tipi even now trying to heal so he could hunt and fight once more.

Survival of the Clan

In order for the government to manage the Indians, whole herds of Buffalo were destroyed. Buffalo carcasses were left to rot on the open plains—completely annihilated. One could no longer witness the magnificent sight of thundering Buffalo herds or see the thick clouds of dust that followed them. It had now become the habit for the armies of the long knives to set themselves upon "the Human Beings" when they had little. When the elders of the council decided to send out a second hunting party, a few braves were chosen. Fresh meat was needed to survive. In every Indian community it was the same. Shamans searched their visions for direction. But as in most "True Ones" communities they were hunted down while desperate ragged and starving and without much needed supplies. So many warriors had been killed or wounded over time that only the youngest and eldest were left to hunt. The feeblest would generally stay behind.

A Decision to be Made

A vote had been taken and agreed upon at tribal council. Three young men, one youth and a boy would be considered for the hunt. The night before the hunting party was to set out, old Tokala Fire Eyes; the shaman and dream interpreter for the tribe, told the council he'd dreamt of a great disturbance. In his dream he'd seen weasels running from their burrows in all directions and birds scattering into the air all at once. He'd seen trees trembling and felt the ground shaking.

"You must wait,"the wise one insisted."I must prepare myself for another vision. It will tell us if this is a good time to leave or not."

The young warriors grumbled. The other members of the tribal council agreed with Tokala Fire Eyes; the hunt should wait. But the impatient young warriors and the new chief, Crazy Bear was insistent upon making the hunt. Crazy Bear's acumen for counting coups (feats of daring) was high. And by the time he was twenty he had already counted over seven.

Crazy Bear was considered hot-headed and reckless according to the elders and was dangerous according to anyone who knew of him. But he was a brave warrior and now had been accepted as chief because of his brother, Strong Hands' recent death. He argued that white-men with pale-faces were taking over and consuming their sacred lands and burial grounds. And he vowed to destroy them swiftly. He saw first-hand how the railroad kept growing in sizeable numbers and strength, cutting off their food supply and restricting their travel. They watched as the Buffalo were shot; slaughtered from railroad cars in order to destroy the lives of the people.

Tokala Fire Eyes was up in age and his health was failing. He tried to get the young warriors to heed the signs of warning from his visions. He was concerned about the outcome. But Crazy Bear was impatient and arrogant. He rejected counsel. He no longer respected the elder's decisions and was skeptical of the shaman's revelations. He insisted that perhaps the old man's visions were incorrect. He didn't want to wait and intended not to heed the old sage's wisdom nor would he talk of peace with a white man. He was restless.

"You're Sani,"Crazy Bear declared to older man; gesturing with his hands.

"The old ways don't work anymore.Your medicine is too weak.Still the white man comes and spreads across our lands like locus, but you want to try to talk of peace with men that have no truth."said Crazy Bear; willfully defiant.

Onawa-Blue-Feather, Kah-La's aunt and Yawns-a-Lot's mother, pleaded with Crazy Bear to heed the advice of the old one.

"Tokala Fire Eyes may be old, but he's wise and is not often wrong.He has always counseled us well. You should listen,"she said, defending the shaman. But Crazy Bear refused to listen. He was determined to do as he pleased and would follow his own counsel. There was nothing anyone could say.

Kah-La Back at the Creek

Kah-La blew his breath into his numbed hands and rubbed them briskly. Nimble fingers would be needed to shoot a bow and arrow when they spotted game—they had to find game. The snow started to fall. Was Coyote taunting them? Kah-La knew that the Great Good Spirit was with them—after all, his father Marcus had survived the impossible. And of the many brave warriors in the village, Marcus was one of the bravest and smartest. Kah-La thought. His father had managed to escape from white man's slavery. But how would he and Yawns-a-Lot escape from this?

Kah-La Remembering...

When he was younger, the other children from the village would often tease Kah-La about his full head of soft woolly hair. His sister Tawa Morning Dance's hair resembled her mothers' and was long and full. But the two siblings had different shaped eyes from the other children. They had broad African noses. Tawa Morning Dance was four years older than her brother, and had matured early as girls often do. She was not easily ruffled by the children's teasing and had quickly learned to shame and repel those who teased her. Her innocence and innate wisdom would often quiet the ramblings of youthful troublemakers, but would sometimes irritate the older women of the village because of it. But the teasing had gotten worse for Kah-La since the death of their mother, Little-Pool-That-Shimmers. His father, Marcus would caution his son to pay no attention to the children's teasing.

"They are children,"Marcus would say."Tell them you belong to this clan just as they do.They are our family and my blood brothers. You must not let their teasing trouble you. You must ignore them."

"But they tease me all the time, father."Kah-La would say angrily.

One day Kah-La finally had had enough of the children's teasing. He went to his father to complain again. "Marcus smiled at his son and shook his head.

"Do you get angry at the rain when it falls upon your head, my son?"asked Marcus.

"No, father,"Kah-La sulked. He knew how his complaint sounded."That is how the Great Good Spirit provides for us,"he replied sulking. Marcus placed a hand upon his young son's shoulder.

"You, my son are being made stronger by their words". "They tease, but their words cannot harm you.Their words cannot prick your skin so that it bleeds,"said Marcus.

"But I do not like their teasing father."Kah-La said animatedly. He kicked a clump of grass.

"My son, there many things we do not like and cannot change; many things that are happening to us now that we have no control of,"said Marcus. He sat and nodded to his son to do the same. Kah-La squat on the ground beside his father and took his knife from its sheath. He furiously began to whittle a stick into a sharp point.

"No one teases you for being different."Kah-La said pouting; he continued to whittle absently. Marcus smiled and looked up at the darkening, summer sky.

"Oh, they laughed at first, my son,"Marcus said nodding. He smiled; remembering.

"But no one laughs at you now, father."Kah-La maintained. He continued to whittle away at the stick in his clenched fist.

"No my son, not now,"said Marcus. A shadow of a smile crossed his lips. He admired the tenacity of his son."After I became one with "The People", my life changed. I am no longer a slave in chains—I am a free man."

Thoughtfully Marcus whispered a quote from a scripture read from a bible that he had heard as a child."It is for freedom that Christ has set us free. Stand firm, then, and do not let yourselves be burdened again by a yoke of slavery."He mumbled imperceptibly.

"What did you say, father".Kah-La asked. Curious;He wondered why his father was mumbling. Marcus watched lovingly as his son fidgeted. But he was a slave he thought. No, he had been a slave he said to himself.

"What did you say, father".The boy asked again. He continued to fidget under the watchful gaze of his father.

"It was an old saying spoken to me by a wise old woman."Marcus spoke slowly.

"But where did you come from, father? How did you get away from your slave-masters?"Kah-La asked; perplexed. He jabbed the sharpened stick into the dirt beside him and re-sheathed his knife. He waited anxiously for his father's answer. Even as a small child, Kah-La was aware of the difference he and his sister shared. He'd heard the stories that different warriors had always told; about seeing slaves in chains; walking behind wagons and held against their will. He was curious about his father's ancestors and the paths they traveled. Marcus rose.

"My son, tomorrow you and I will ride to Eagle Rock Falls to gather flint and stones for our arrows and knives.Then I will tell you my story."Marcus could no longer keep from the boy the horror of what he had lived thru. And the long ride would give him time to consider how to tell his son what he had endured to become a free man and what the circumstances were, that led him to be with "their people".

The Journey to Eagle Rock Falls

The following morning the women had packed the ponies with dried foods and supplies for the long journey. It was several days' ride from their hidden encampment to gather flint. The flint and stones that Marcus and Kah-La would bring back would be fashioned into useful tools and weapons. The falls had been a favored destination for all clans; a place to fish and swim and to enjoy. The gathering of flint rock had usually been a woman's task, but Marcus wanted to spend time with his son. Marcus and Kah-La would spend several nights on lands that were becoming the territories of white bureaucrats.

Their Arrival at the Falls

It was early evening when the pair finally reached their destination. They watched for any signs of the enemy.Marcus surveyed their surroundings and the two dismounted. The waning sun crept behind the clouds and winked out of sight. In contemplative silence, the pair guided their ponies to the creek and found a small clearing. They made a small campfire while listening to the sounds that the forest made around them. Kah-La stood beside the edge of the creek and listened to the rushing waterfall. It glinted and sparkled against the fading light and cascaded into a pool of white foam. The smell of moss and the film of mist filled the air. They were tired from the long ride. But Marcus was anxious. This was a critical time to be away from the others. He prepared a small fire and sat cross legged on his blanket. He observed as his son copied him and handed the boy a piece of jerky. Tomorrow they would get up early to gather flint and track game they could bring back to their families. Tonight he would prepare his son.

Marcus' Story

Marcus set a piece of jerky between his teeth and was thoughtful. He pulled his robes around him and watched the fire crackle and sizzle.

"I was born on a plantation far away from here.I don't know the year and I don't know my exact age. I was a kennel man. I got the dogs ready for the hunts."Marcus lifted his voice above the roaring waterfall and watched the flames dance.

"What is a plantation, father?" young Kah-La asked, lifting his voice too. He sat clutching his knees to his chest, anticipating his father's story. Marcus cleared his throat.

"It is a place where white men and their families live and work and own livestock, and beat the slaves they own." He said with venom.Marcus continued." Slaves do most of the work on plantations." He said sarcastically.

"The slave owner and tobacco farmer was also my father." He said angrily; hesitant. Kah-La frowned; curious. Marcus continued.

"I never knew my mother; I was told her name was Melissa by the old woman who raised me.She told me about my mother and said she was in fact my grandmother—my mother's mother."

"What was your grandmother's name father?" Kah-La asked;probing. He was anxious to know why his own father would treat him that way; but was afraid to ask.

"They called her Sarah. In Hebrew it means lady, she died not long after the old master did—she was the only person that I ever cared for and the only person that ever cared for me." Marcus said sadly. "My grandmother named me. In Greek my name means warlike. We had no last name except the master's and I will never speak that evil man's name—that was his name not mine,"Marcus said glaring; outrage stinging his eyes. He bent down and picked up a stone.

In one breath, Kah-La wanted to ask what Lady and Hebrew and Greek meant, but the fire that flashed in his fathers' eyes halted his inquisitive voice.

"What happened to your mother, father?" The boy asked instead; his mouth filled with jerky. Marcus pondered fully; Kah-La's question as he sat up and stirred the fire. He watched his son pick up and examine a stone in the shadows of firelight.

"She died." But when I was your age I use to hear the slave women tell stories about my mama—about her beauty.They said she was a pretty little thing.They said master had his eye on her when she was very young,"explained Marcus.

"To keep my mama safe; the older women would offer themselves to him to try to keep him away from her at least till she was older. They hid her when they'd see the drunken master coming but he knew where she was.They said master was always sniffing around looking for her or he'd send someone else around to keep an eye on his property. The women protected her as long as they could." Marcus said gripping his robe with balled fist.

"One day when the master was drunk, he came for her and took her.Some of the women tried to tell him she was too young, they tried to protect her. But master didn't care.He had all the women beaten that day.And then he sent away for a contraption that the women had to wear over their heads and mouths.They wore them till their mouths would bleed and their skin was rubbed raw." Marcus said trying to contain his anger.

Kah-La started to interrupt Marcus to ask more questions. He wanted to know what a contraption was. He could sense his father's rage. He didn't interrupt.

"The master had the women fitted with iron muzzles that had locks on them so they couldn't talk or eat or drink," said Marcus.And he kept my mother locked in a room in the main house so he could do what he wanted with her.Her body was too small to bear a child and survive.But he didn't care—he killed my mother—and she bled to death giving birth to me,"Marcus said standing. He shook his head and clenched his fist.

Kah-La listened; wide eyed. Marcus rose to gather more wood for their fire, and to think. Kah-La followed his father's lead and helped to gather wood too. He realized his father Marcus had never known his mother—and had never been held by her. He cringed at the very idea of anyone having to wear an iron muzzle on their face. He felt the deep sense of loss for his own mother. They gathered in silence. Their ponies stirred at their movements. They needed rest but he continued with his story once he was seated again and the fire was stirred.

"I was bred to be a slave and I was meant to die a slave,"continued Marcus. "That's all I knew.I never knew what it would be like to be free, but I know now as a free man that I will never be a slave for any man again,"Marcus said resolutely. Kah-La stood beside his father wanting to somehow comfort him. Holding his head high; Marcus drew a breath and filled his lungs with the sweet smell of wet pine and rotting wood, Marcus Buffalo's Heart Long Bow was resigned to endure his freedom with his family—for as long as he lived.

"We must get rest. It will be dawn too soon." Marcus said rolling onto his blanket and covering himself with his buffalo robe. Kah-La followed suit.

"Will you tell me the rest of your story tomorrow?" Kah-La asked. He snuggled beneath his robe and fell asleep before his father could answer.

They were up with the sun the following morning. The two followed the riverbed into a thicket of huge trees. Marcus stood six foot five and was the color of sand. Kah-La felt great pride for his father—who was tall and strong and muscular. The boy wondered if he would grow up to be like him. He watched his father move gracefully; nimbly leaping from stone to stone back to shore. Kah-La followed in his father's footsteps. They collected different sizes of flint stones and stuffed them into their leather pouches. Marcus continued to retell his son his story while they collected.

"Slaves are white man's property, like the animals they owned. We were never meant to be free men as long a white man could own us." Marcus spoke with distain." They whipped us like animals. Full grown men beaten for no reason at all—just so they could control the women."

They somberly gathered more stones and filled several pouches and laid them aside.

"What do you mean, father? How would they control the women?" Kah-La asked—his eyes widening. He followed his father; navigating the rocks in the swirling waters. Marcus said nothing for quite a while; thinking his way thru the painful details. They listened for any other signs of movement—or human life that might be approaching. When they heard nothing but the winds and the water; Marcus spoke again.

"Mothers tried to protect their children from terrible things that the white men does." He said looking up at the sky between the leaves of the trees.

"Their animals were better off than we were,"He said; studying the face of his naïve son. Marcus glanced away.

Kah-La swallowed." Why didn't your father take care of you?" Kah-La asked innocently. The boy would learn soon enough about white man's culture.

"Even though he was my father—he was a slave owner and I was his slave. I was treated the worst because he knew that I had been told that he was my father. And the other slaves made certain I'd never forget I was his son, either. The grandmother couldn't do anything to protect me, she was a slave too, and old." Marcus said matter-of-factly—but his stirred memories began to enrage him. He motioned to his son to follow him. With the pouches now filled with stones; they cleared the water and sat cross-legged on the ground. Marcus pulled a piece of jerky from his pouch and handed it to his son, thoughtfully.

"Most of the slaves treated me bad.Some of them beat me and spat on me.Most of the men took turns—doing all kinds of terrible things to me because I was the master's son.Some did even worse." He said closing his eyes; shaking his head." They took it out on me because they knew—the master wouldn't help me." Marcus said lowering his head. Kah-La didn't want to know what the men did to his father. He knew that whatever it was, was beyond telling.

"I learned to hate him and he hated me. And in a ways I think he liked having me to take his beatings from the slaves that hated him, because he didn't have to." Marcus said recalling what had been done.

"I was his sacrifice—his seed." Marcus said with venom.

"How did you end up becoming a Human Being, father?" Kah-La asked gently; when his father became quiet—lost in his thoughts.

"Only with the help of the Great Good Spirit—or Coyote,"said Marcus—trying to change the tone of his anger. He shrugged then winked at the boy.

"We must eat"said Marcus. It was late afternoon. The two would spend another night at the falls. Marcus would tell his young son all of what was challenging his memories. It would be a long story.

Marcus and Kah-La followed the rabbits they'd seen, leaving the ponies to graze. They finally returned to camp with a rabbit each. They skinned them both and began to roast them over the newly made fire. Kah-La was still eager to hear more of his father's ordeal. He would wait.

Marcus had been silent. He needed courage to repeat his story to his son. He felt a deep sadness and sense of regret; to be so despised and hated by a people with pale skin.Did the white men feel they were a superior race? Their actions have only shown that they were not.

The two sat and watched the rabbits roast while the colors of the horizon changed. Marcus began slowly in the retelling of his steps in becoming a "Human Being".

"I almost died back then.Burning wagons—people dying—a massacre." Marcus heaved a sigh from the weight of the story he hadn't ever shared. He fell silent again—listening to the calm swirling waters off in the distance and snap and sizzle of the warm and gentle fire in front of them—soothing him. His memories of that raging fire so long ago was seared behind his eyes.

"Tell me father, I want to know what happened,"insisted Kah-La who was anxious to hear all that his father had to say. Marcus drew a deep breath. He continued:

"When the Master died, all his property was sold at auction to another slave owner. We were sent to pick cotton for a season and then we were sold again to somebody else who took us to another slave auction. When slaves are sold, we're stripped naked and made to stand on a big wooden block in front of white men in fine clothes." Marcus turned the roasting meat over, the scent of it rising into the air, the fat of it dripping into the noisy fire. Their stomachs grumbled with hunger.

"We were examined all over—they looked at our teeth and hands and feet to make sure we were healthy and strong; much in the way I would examine a horse or dog. Even the women were naked and examined in front of the men—those white men shamed us all. One day several of us was picked to go to another plantation to work. I was sure glad I would never have to ever see them slaves I had known all my life. We worked for several plantations and then one day four of us were taken with a wagon train. We didn't know where we were going. We had no shoes or clothes to keep us warm." Marcus said remembering.

"We were tied together by heavy iron bands around our necks, hands and feet. We were shackled in chains; in—chains to the wagons," Marcus said vehemently. Marcus caught himself flinching involuntarily. The newly re-surfaced memories caught him off guard.

29

"The wagon Master was Benjamin Oliver.Lawd, that man was mean.He was the meanest white man on earth." Marcus smiled remembering. He shook his head.

"He was a brutal; fat, white man that Plantation owners hired to buy and trade slaves for them.And he got rich from slave trading. Slaves were being worked to death.And black men were being kidnapped and sold into slavery." Marcus said sadly.

The wind had shifted. Dusk had fallen upon them. A snap of a twig echoed in the distance. Marcus raised a hand; Kah-La didn't move but strained to hear what his father was listening to. Moments later they observed a family of four deer across the creek that had come to drink. They smelled the food. Marcus' first instinct was to hunt and bring fresh meat back to camp but if he moved at all, the animals would be gone before he reached his weapon and their food would probably be burned; instead they waited until the animals had gone before resuming their talk—they could track them.

Marcus removed the roasted meat and placed them on rocks that his son had previously cleaned. Kah-La ate. Marcus couldn't.

"Back then, after the grandmother died; I never got close to anyone again; I didn't want to.You couldn't make friends; you better not.Too many folks trying to win favor with the master... they'd tell everything." Marcus shrugged absently.

"You couldn't marry and have children.Oh, some tried. But anyone you cared about would be snatched away from you by the master when he found out, and he always found out.There was always somebody wanting to be favored by the master." Marcus said.

"We learned that Oliver and two other men were always taking slaves along with them whenever they were driving settlers to new lands. They knew they could sell us to somebody somewhere." Marcus went on; he glanced at Kah-La who tossed the bones into the fire to burn. He ran to the creek, washed off his hands and sat back pulling his blanket around him. His belly was full. Soon he would be asleep. But Kah-La didn't fall asleep as quickly as Marcus thought. He was wide awake waiting for his father to continue. He waited and listened to his father breathe.Marcus saw the opened eyes of his son looking up at the stars—so Marcus continued.

"The wagon train left in the fall when the nights were getting coolest.We'd sleep on the ground with nothing.We were kept cold and hungry.A few times somebody gave us some ole feed bags to cover ourselves with, but we they weren't enough, we couldn't get warm."

"That mean ole white man wouldn't let us keep them bags and he whipped us every day so's we were afraid." Marcus sighed. He didn't try to hide his contempt and anger from his son.

A Decision to Read

He rose and refilled the skin pouch in the creek. He knew the boy would sooner or later have to deal with his own emotions in his own way someday. He'd have to learn about the white man's ways. Marcus knew his son's destiny depended on it. It was going to be almost impossible because "The people" were already suffering. What kind of life would Kah-La have? His son was of two of the most hated people on earth like himself. Who would accept him? What would life be for his children's children? Kah-La had to learn to read the white man's words, he decided.

"Father?" Kah-La urged; chewing.

Marcus was deep in thought. How long would coyote let the white man reign havoc over their lives? Did the God that his grandmother prayed to and believed in, really want this sadness for her children?Marcus worried. Marcus remembered the old well-worn bible that Sarah kept wrapped and hidden in the floorboards of the cabin where he was housed as a slave. Where was it now? He wondered. Marcus never told anyone that Sarah had taught him to read. It was their secret.

"Father?" Kah-La asked again shaking his father from his thoughts.

"Sarah would read the passages from the Bible whenever she could sneak it out from under its hiding place.It was against the law for slaves to read.But the masters' wife wasn't as smart as the grandmother, and when she realized how smart my grandmother was she insisted that Sarah knew how to run the kitchen, the house and correct the books on the plantation... that means keep a tally of what was bought and sold and what supplies were needed and if she made a mistake, she was beaten severely for it". "She knew the importance of reading." He had no idea how the impossible would be achieved but Marcus needed to find books for his son.

Marcus held up the animal skin pouch and drank from it deeply. He held out the contents to his sleepy son. He observed Kah-La's features as the boy accepted the skin and drank. Yes, Kah-La would have to learn to read and decipher the talking papers of the white man. Marcus continued to tell the story well into the night and Kah-La watched the stars and listened.

"The wagon train had been traveling for a few days when four of us tried to escape. Oliver caught us. And he beat us real bad, and then he put the chains on our necks."Marcus said smiling, and then he was serious." He branded our feet with a hot iron to keep us from trying to escape again—he threatened to poke out our eyes but he knew he'd get nothing for blind slaves.Branding our feet slowed us down. But we were slaves and Oliver wouldn't let us ride in the wagons."

"The Humans kept their distance but they watched us; making everyone afraid.Eventually they surrounded and overtook us in the middle of the night when the watchman fell asleep.Oliver knew we were outnumbered. He was more afraid than anyone.But in punishing us he destroyed all chances of us getting away safely, we had to make a stand.That fat man was huffing and sweating, and ordering everybody to overturn the wagons.And while the settlers ducked behind the wagons, we slaves were pushed out in front to be killed first." Marcus said shrugging his shoulders.

"The Indians was whoopin' and hollerin' and shooting flaming arrows at us.They setthe wagons on fire. I didn't know how we were ever going live to see another day.I didn't think we ever would.I prayed harder than I ever prayed before,"said Marcus; placing twigs in the small fire.

"Four of us slaves were chained to a wagon that belonged to a young white doctor named Matthew Warwick.He was a good man and kinder than most white folks I ever met.But we were all trying to crouch behind the burning wagon to keep from getting shot, and then the slave that never talked got hit in the neck by an arrow and died right in front of us.The next thing I saw was Smithy. He'd been hit in the leg with an arrow.Then Matthew, the doctor was shot and an arrow was sticking out of his chest."

35

"What is a doctor, father?"asked Kah-La. The gruesome details of his father's story no longer seemed to faze him. He digested the words of his father's story along with the roasted rabbit he had eaten.

"A Doctor is not unlike our medicine man, son."answered Marcus. He noticed his son's resolve. As Marcus told his story, he found it more and more difficult to recall anything pleasant to his memory but to tell the story as he had lived it. Having to use words and names that his son did not understand was tedious, but he continued...

"Matthew was holding onto his gun with his doctor's bag next to him.He tried to speak and he pointed to his doctor's bag.But blood was gurgling out of his mouth and chest.He knew we didn't stand a chance chained up like that.He knew he was dying. And with his last breath, he did what no other white man would ever to do.He motioned to his doctor's bag and held his gun out to us."Marcus said gesturing.

"But it was just out of Big John's reach.The flames leaped at our clothing.We was scared we were going to burn to death.We all pulled as hard as we could to move that wagon.So we could reach the bag and the gun.Beyond us people were screaming and dying and being scalped and killed—everything was on fire and burning and smoking.It was a terrible, terrible thing."Marcus said; shaking his head."It was awful."

"Then all at once the burning wagon we was chained to rolled, just a little.Big John twisted his big body around and pushed that gun towards me with his foot, I grabbed the gun and felt the hot metal of the barrel and started banging the gun against the lock on our chains.It was burning my hands,"Explained Marcus excitedly. Kah-La's eyes were glued to his father's face as his father told of his past.

"Shoot the lock!, Shoot the lock! Big John was screaming at me over the roar of them burning hot flames.I...I never fired a gun.I never even held one in my hands.I couldn't hear what Big John was saying." I just kept beating the lock with the gun like it was a hammer.Finally I found the trigger. I pointed the gun at the lock and shot it and it opened, just as the clothes of the dead slave caught fire.Big John grabbed the doctor's bag and pushed himself away from the wagon.Smithy was wounded and was bleeding, but we managed to crawl after Big John, dragging the body of the dead slave behind us.We kept praying that the Humans wouldn't pay any attention to us,"said Marcus in a rush of breath.

Eyes wide; Kah-La looked at his father in horror. "What is a hammer, father?"Kah-La asked; curious.

"Big John and I brought some tools with us when we came to the village.It's what the white men use to build with." It's the one with the metal head and wooden handle."It was one of the tools that your mother took a liking to.She wanted it and she took it."Marcus remembered fondly.

"Oh,"said the little warrior; his eyes wide. Kah-La knew that the tool was; now a prized possession of his sister; Tawa Morning Dance. Kah-La's mind was racing; filled with thoughts of what his father must have gone through.

"For a long time we just sat and waited and listened to the dying people moaning."Marcus said sadly. He closed his eyes and could still see the images in his head. He remembered the sounds; the smell. He shook his head, and looked at his son.

"The fire was so hot our hair and skin was singed; our clothes were burned."Marcus said gesturing. "We crawled away from the burning wagons; covered with blisters and blood.The hair in our nostrils smelled like burning and death too,"said Marcus. He stared into the bright flames.

"There was nothing we could do."Marcus finally said.

"Nothing but wait till the Humans came to kill us too.We couldn't run, not with Smithy bleeding and a corpse attached to us holding us back.We had a gun, but so did them white people, but they died.We thought we were going to die too and there wasn't anything else we could do except wait.All we could do is hope the humans didn't kill us.So we waited and we listened.And when the humans didn't come for us we waited till everyone was dead and the fire was almost out before we went back to search for the keys.It was the worst thing I'd ever seen in my life."Marcus said pained.

"It is difficult to tell you these things—to share with you the terrible things these eyes have seen, my son,"said Marcus.

"But you must tell me Father,"urged Kah-La.

"But—it is difficult to remember these things, my son,"Marcus said; staring out at the changing sky. He said nothing for a long time.

"I did not want you to know any of this until I thought you were ready."said Marcus rising to make water. Kah-La followed.

"But it is our story father, and I am ready."

"Someday I will no longer be young and I plan to share my stories with my sons, Father.You must tell me your story so I can tell it to my sons' and they can pass it on to their sons at Pow-Wows."Kah-La said fearlessly. He sat back down waiting for his father. Kah-La was nine seasons old.

Marcus nodded and looked away—proud. He squinted at the clouds in the colored sky.

"It felt like an eternity."Marcus said warily.

"What is an eter-nity?"asked Kah-La; his eyes filled with wonder. He studied his father's face. Kah-La was curious. He was learning new words he had rarely heard spoken—English, the language of his father's past.

"What is an eter-nity?"Kah-La asked again. Marcus looked out; watching the changing sky. He tried to relax.

"Eternity is Coyote doing everything to make our lives as miserable as he can and never ceasing."He said chuckling. "It feels like forever.We were in the fires of hell."Marcus said softly; almost whispering.

Kah-La nodded as if he understood—perhaps he did. Some day he would. Marcus was determined to get through the worst of his story.

"The smell of human flesh being burned made us sick.We dragged and pulled ourselves away from the heat.It was bad.Smithy knew he was dying but he was happy he would die a free man.One warrior saw us—three strange woolly haired men in chains; crawling along the ground, dragging a dead man. But he left us alone—he had no quarrel with us."Marcus said.

"What happened, father,"asked Kah-La.

"My son you must understand that I can never be a slave again—no man should ever be a slave to another man.We must live as free men and die as free men. We must be one with the land and sky. We must respect the animal spirits—we must respect this land." Marcus said determined.

"We must respect each other." said Kah-La speaking up. Marcus nodded.

"I will never live as a slave again. That is no life for a man." Marcus said slowly. He knew he would die first. Kah-La mirrored his fathers' gesture.

"I will never be a slave, either father," The boy said firmly. Marcus became quiet; reminiscing; he stirred and added more twigs to the dwindling fire and listened to call of animals in the distance. Kah-La interrupted the silence.

"Father, will you tell me about Big John?" he asked. Marcus nodded and continued..."I will tell you more tomorrow, my son. I must rest," he said stirring the coals of the fire again.

Kah-La looked disappointed but, he was tired as well. It had been a long day of digesting the stories of his father... and he became frightened. Kah-La soon fell asleep. Marcus couldn't sleep; he stood and listened to the hush and echo of splashing water off the falls.

The Second Day at Eagle Rock Falls

All night Marcus rehearsed what he was going to tell his son. He had little sleep. Kah-La jumped up; made water, rolled up his bedding up, setting it aside. He sat beside the already made fire where his father sat waiting for him. He handed the boy a piece of jerky and started telling the rest of the story.

"Big John was responsible for the butchering of the livestock on the plantation where he was held. He knew what he had to do to set us free.He took the bone saw from the doctor's bag."Marcus said slowly; he glanced over at his son then spoke:

"I had one bullet left in the gun; I held it in both hands. I shut one eye, and shot the lock on the chain at the dead man's waist.Smithy was no use.I had to help hold the body of the slave up, so Big John could remove the rest of his body from the chains."

"You mean the way we skin the buffalo, father?"asked Kah-La frowning. His mouth was full. His curious eyes were wide.

"Well, not exactly,"said Marcus gently. He looked away and closed his eyes. This was a story he only relived in his nightmares. It wasn't one he'd ever wanted to share with his children—especially his children. Being a slave was not an option. It was not a life for anyone. Marcus watched his son as he continued to tell him of the life he had lived. Marcus

bit off a piece of jerky and chewed slowly—
thoughtfully. Leaving their camp, they climbed
aboard their ponies and traveled further to collect
more flint along the creek bed. A ways from their
campsite they silently scrounged and collected the
flint they needed. They searched and collected well
into sunny midday; always listening. Marcus decided
to walk the ponies back to the camp so that he could
talk and listen to the winds and the animals.

Marcus spoke softly; remembering of how Big John
had to remove the head and other parts of the body
from the chains they wore as slaves. He remembered
the horror."We was scared; sitting in those heavy
chains, with our backs against the trees; just shaking
and bleeding.We couldn't run.Smithy was dying.Big
John was shaking when he took the bone saw out of
the doctor's bag."Kah-La listened intently. Wild
eyed and horrified.

"We couldn't, I—I—couldn't think about what we
were doing—what we had to do to get out of those
chains.We'd be dead men today if we hadn't done
what we had to do."Marcus said struggling to find
the words to explain his gruesome story. Eyeing the
landscape, Marcus felt the winds shift then relaxed.

"Smithy was just about done for; we had already
broken off the arrow that was stuck in his leg.We
had to get free of them chains."

Wide eyed; Kah-La listened, fully understanding the weight of his father's story and accepting what his father had to do to be able to stand before him now.

"We were free from the body of the dead man but not free of the chains.And we were covered in a lot of blood…"Marcus said; trembling at the memory.

"Blood was everywhere.Thanked the Great Good Spirit; that the Humans didn't try to stop us. And I thanked the God of my grandmother, too.The humans paid us little mind.We were scared, in pain.Our skin was burned, blistered and raw. We smelled like smoke,"said Marcus clenching his jaw.

Again Marcus repeated;"For a long time we could hear the screams and moans of the dying.Men, women, children were being killed all around us.We could smell their flesh burning.And after all the fighting and killing, the Human Beings made off with the ponies and all the supplies they could take.And when the screams and moaning stopped, Big John, Smithy and I were alone and the Human Beings were gone."

"By then it was dark.The wagons were smoking and every one of those white people was dead.Big John carried Smithy and we stumbled and clanked them chains back to where the wagons were burning to find them keys.It was too dark to make out who was male or female, child or adult.The smell..."Marcus put his hands over his mouth; he remembered visually.

"People were roasted like meat."Marcus said slowly. "I will never forget the sounds...what I saw, no one should ever see—It made us—sick to our stomachs.Smithy kept laughing and muttering to himself; "I's free, I's a free man.I's goin ta die a free man an go to heaven.But we still had to find them keys to get us free,"Marcus said emphatically.

"Big John and I had to work as quickly as we could before them animals' smelled death and came looking for food.And finding them keys to our chains was our only chance to run and be free."Marcus explained to his attentive son.

"Smithy just kept smiling and saying through his pain;It's all right…I knows I am dyin'. I'm just glad to be dying a free man…yes'sa…a free man!I am a free man and the taste of freedom is sweet."Marcus said smiling; remembering the words of his old friend.

"It was almost light when we finally found the charred remains of Oliver's body—he was impaled, and scalped.And there; burned from his belt and shining under his wagon wheels were the keys to our chains...keys to freedom."Marcus said; triumphantly.

"Big John and I unshackled ourselves and helped Smithy out of his chains.Smithy was almost dead and was barely breathing.Big John carried Smithy back to the edge of the woods to rest, and gave him some water to drink.While I kept looking for supplies and anything else I could find to keep us.We knew Smithy wasn't gonna make it, but he was happy anyways.He bled almost to death, but he was happy to die a free man."Marcus bragged.

"Me and Big John wanted Smithy to be as comfortable as he could be before he died being a free man." said Marcus. Kah-La listened in awe as his father shared with him, the story of his life before he came to live with the "true ones".

"At first we found some charred cloth and a few feed bags that hadn't burned... We put the body of the slave who'd been chained with us into one of the feed bags."Marcus said; recalling the details.

"Smithy was right. For the first time in our lives, we could all taste the breath of freedom, even if it was for one precious moment.We could somehow imagine a time when we would never again have our skin seared by a hot branding iron or when we would never again be beaten with whips or set in chains or have to witness our women and young girls being raped by white men.Or have dogs set upon us."

"For one brief moment we could fill our thoughts of a future when we wouldn't have to see anyone wearing an iron muzzle or stand helpless while mothers screamed in agony because their children were ripped from their arms; or watch a slaver maim a man for no reason.Sometimes an old slave was beaten to death because he couldn't work anymore, or they sicced the dogs on him to remind all the slaves of what they had coming.Sometimes slaves were beaten because they dared to look a white man in the eye, or if they were caught laughing."said Marcus; enraged; his fist balled.

"And sometimes slaves were beaten and bloodied till their skin was raw because a white man thought it was funny.We all dreamed of a time where we could smile and be happy for...for no reason at all!"Marcus said wistfully. The two arrived back at camp and unloaded the heavy pouches. They ate their dried rations too tired to hunt at first.

It would never be easy for any one that did not share the skin color of the white man. They would always see themselves as superior to anyone no matter what the Bible of God said.

Marcus stopped to listen to the sounds of the winds whistling through the trees; waiting—hearts pounding. Any movement in their surroundings could mean danger—be it animal or enemy. Kah-La was a child but knew to be attentive as well; all children did. After a long tense moment Kah-La whispered. Cautious; Marcus motioned for his son to keep still.

"Father, is the iron muzzle, a contraption?"Kah-La asked; baffled by all the new things that his father was sharing with him. "Yes."Marcus answered.

"The iron muzzle was mostly used on the women-folk and when they defended my mother."

"Oh."Kah-La replied; imagining what it must have looked like.

"Big John always said he would never go back to being a slave.That he'd kill any man trying to capture him or he would die trying.And he said he'd kill me too if I ever tried to surrender.So we gathered up ax heads, shovels, hammer heads and anything else we could find that we could carry to use or trade with and we shoved everything in two feed bags.We didn't find much in the way of clothes or food; a few cans of beans and some dried jerky.I found the pouch of silver coins that Oliver hid in the water barrel and I buried it too—inside the doc's bag,"said Marcus pensively.

"Why didn't you keep the pouch with the silver coins, father?"Kah-La asked surprised.

"Because we knew that someone somewhere would have a list of all the slaves on that wagon train and I knew we couldn't afford to be caught with that money.We couldn't get caught with anything we took, especially that money, that money was tainted,"said Marcus grimacing.

"No good could ever come from tainted money—
money that paid for the lives of slaves.And no white
man would ever believe a white doctor gave us his
gun before he died.We knew we had to find those
keys because when the bodies of those people were
found, there'd be a hunting party to look for any
Human Beings,Even if they had nothing to do with
the death of those settlers.And if we were ever found
alive—we'd be strung up just for being alive—and
blamed for what happened to the people on the
wagon train.The white man needed to think we were
captured or dead too."Marcus said fiercely.

"Why does the white man want to take everything
that does not belong to him?"Kah-La asked annoyed.

"You see my son, that this is his true nature—to
take." The white man has nohonor.My grandmother
was taught to read to the white man's children too.It
was against the law for a slave to read but the master
had her read the white man's books". "She was
smart; she caught on quickly when she was little.She
learned to read faster than anybody knew she could,
and she never let on that she read as good as she
did.One book she loved to read to us was that
Bible.And in it, it speaks of slaves.It also speaks of
us being free in my grandmother's bible; in
Galatians 5 and 1." We're not to be tangled again
with the yoke of bondage.It also says something
about us all being equal men and that God will
render to each man according to his deeds."Quoted
Marcus.

49

Kah-La had become mesmerized by his father Marcus's life. The boy beamed. He was quite proud of his brave father. He was in awe of his father's telling of the terrible life that his father had left to become a Human Being. The tragedy of what Marcus had experienced and lived through was something that Marcus now wanted to protect his son from. And it tore at his heart. The known truths about the true savages.

"What's a bible and who is God, and what is a gal-a-tan five and one?" Kah-La asked; rushing the words out—almost all in one breath. The boy was indeed spellbound by the new things he was hearing his father speak of.

Marcus took in a very deep breath and drank in deeply the sweet smell of the air about him... and for now; freedom.

"Father?" Kah-La pleaded. Marcus smiled and sighed.

"God's the Great Good Spirit, son. But white men says our kind isn't human and we should be beaten and treated like we are worse than the animals they own." Marcus said gently. There were many things that his young son wanted to know but Kah-La could only absorb so much and that perhaps his story would need to be repeated and remembered in time.

Kah-La grew quiet and sighed."What happened after you and Big John found the keys?"he asked curious.

"Me and Big John draped those sets of shackles and chains over our shoulders, an carried the sack of supplies back to where we left Smithy—we found him dead; slumped against a tree—with a smile on his face."

"We never knew the dead slave's name.We put his body in one of the feed bags and carried both bodies to the opposite side of the creek and dug a deep enough grave so's no animal could reach 'em. We wanted to bury 'em proper.Both men were in a better place than the one they left."Marcus said with conviction.

"An with the coming dawn, me and Big John buried two bodies along with the chains and shackles, the doctors bag and the leather pouch full of money.We covered the single grave with heavy stones and rotting logs."Marcus watched a hawk circle above their heads and smiled.

"My son, are you not hungry?" Marcus asked; his stomach grumbling. The dried meat made him hungrier. He had not eaten as much as his son did the night before. And had wrapped the other rabbit in wet leaves and left it in the coals to smoke.

"Yes, father, let's hunt. I'm hungry." Kah-La said nodding. The two took off to hunt for more rabbits.

And to do that they had to be in complete silence. When they got back, they prepared the rabbit as they had done the day before.Marcus examined the dried rabbit left in the coals and sat back while Kah-La rested his elbows on his knees; face in hands, he watched the meat roast.

"I never did tell Big John about the money in the pouch,"said Marcus wryly. Kah-La frowned.

"Why didn't you tell him, father?"Kah-La asked curious. Marcus just shook his head.

"I couldn't. It wouldn't make no difference.We were starving, scared and desperate and slaves.That tainted money wasn't going to buy us our freedom.I couldn't tell him about the pouch; it would have made everything worse.Big John always told me what he would do if he had money, but that money would have gotten us both dead if we were found with any of it."

"We were slaves, not free men—even though Big John was a free man once.Money is the reason why we're slaves in the first place.Greed's the reason why the people are losing their lands.White men didn't ask the "humans beings" if they wanted to be pushed from their lands.Their nature demands that they control everything or destroy everything they touch."

"So once, me and Big John got ourselves free we said a prayer that we wouldn't ever get caught again.We washed ourselves up in the creek to get the stink of blood and smoke off us.Then we covered our bodies with mud and moss because we were blistered so badly.We even put the mud in our hair and on our clothes because we were covered in so much blood we couldn't stand to see it ourselves."Marcus stopped and took a deep breath; rubbing his beard. It was a painful memory andthen we got away from there as fast as we could,"said Marcus reflectively.

"We had a better chance to live free with the "Humans Beings" than be on our own as runaway slaves.And we'd rather be dead than slaves ever again.But to our good fortune, it started to rain—hard.The rain would hide our tracks—at least for a while.And we were glad the creek would help us hide."Kah-La listened quietly to his father.

"For weeks we stayed close to the creek, zigzagging back and forth to throw off our scent. Just in case someone came looking for us.It didn't matter much because we got sprayed by a skunk, when we stumbled onto his home."Marcus said smiling. He winked at his son.Kah-La wrinkled his nose.

"Me and Big John kept ourselves alive by eating anything we could—not much more than what we'd been given to eat when we was slaves.One night we slipped past a military camp of a dozen or so white men.Since we were no longer traveling with a wagon train, we were no longer privy to the common talk and rumors.We could only guess at what they were talking about.We crept past them as quiet as ghost and smelling like skunk.And folks don't go looking for skunks."Marcus said; scratching his head. He rubbed his beard and smiled.

"I'd grown up a slave, but Big John had been a free man.He said he came from a place called Sierra Leone.It's a country in Africa."Marcus said anticipating his son's question. He turned the roasting rabbit.

"Big John was a merchant of spices and came to see the world.What a sight he ended up seeing.He'd only been here four or five moons before he was kidnapped, robbed, beaten and sold into slavery.He found no one with dark skin was free here."

"How did you know "the people" would take you in father?"Kah-La asked; his stomach grumbled.

"We didn't know if the Human Beings would take us in or kill us, but we had little choice other than to find them—any of them, we were not going back!"Marcus insisted.

"We showed up in our ragged, muddy clothes and stinking like skunk."Marcus laughed remembering what they must have looked and smelled like to the Humans.

"It was Quick Eye, who saw us first.He recognized us from the wagon train even thru the mud."Marcus chuckled.

"When we got close to the people they were all holdin' their noses, the dogs ran away as fast as their legs could take them and even the ponies backed away from us."Marcus threw his head back and laughed out loud.

"We were a sight.And we stank—as bad as an un-washed enemy." Marcus said laughing.Kah-La threw his head back and laughed too.

"Was Quick Eye one of the warriors that was killed before I was born, father?"Kah-La asked.

"Quick Eye was one of the first brave warriors I met.And yes, they tell his story at the Pow-Wows.Quick-Eye was impressed that we survived being chained to a burning wagon,"said Marcus smiling."…and so were we."

"Why didn't they help you get away, father?"Kah-La asked; licking his lips at the cooking meat. Hunger had stirred his appetite.

"That wasn't their way, my son—they left us alone.It was up to us to us to get away, if we were going to live.Some of the other warriors were suspicious of us when we first showed up; others were impressed that we wanted to join with them.Pretty soon we found ourselves face to face with a whole line of angry warriors surrounding us.Women and children were pointing and laughing at us—dogs were growling and snapping at us."said Marcus chuckling. He removed the meat from the spit and divvied it up. Kah-La ate slowly...thinking.

"We didn't back down, even though we were scared to death.We didn't speak their language and we didn't budge.Big John stood nose to nose with the biggest warrior—his name was Odakota-Dark-Cloud.And after a heated debate between warriors, the village elders decided to let us stay on."Marcus said with a mouth full of meat.

"The women ushered us to a creek to bathe first and they gave us some skin rags to wash with.It took a long time to wash all that stink and mud off.We'd been wearin' it for a long time.Then they gave us some blankets to cover ourselves with". "Then we were allowed to eat—away from them, of course,"laughed Marcus.

"You and Big John didn't mind them laughing at you, father?"Kah-La asked; his mouth full.

"No, my son, their laughter was a welcomed sound to our ears." The women fixed us hot bowls of corn soup, all the while laughin' at us.I don't think I ever tasted anythin' as good as that soup before."

"Did it have a Buffalo's head in it too father?"asked the boy

Marcus smiled at his inquisitive son,"Yes my son, it did and sometime later—a few weeks maybe, Big John and I showed the Humans Beings where we hid the supplies we brought with us."

"Why didn't you bring the supplies with you?"Kah-La asked; curious. He tossed the last of the bones into the fire.

"You see me and Big John didn't know what to expect.We didn't know what we were walking into, so we made a decision to show up empty handed.But then after we saw how Human Beings shared with each other, we decided it was alright to share our supplies with our new family.Human Beings are big on sharing and they don't ever mind sharing what they have, but, just don't try to take nothing from them,"said Marcus winking.

"When it was time to move on, we moved north and west, even moving deep into Dakota Territory.As moons passed, we learned to communicate with the Human Beings by learning the language.And we learned the ways of the warriors and how to hunt.We learned how they use the buffalo for nearly everything.And we taught them a few words here and there.We scouted, hunted, fished and fought together as free men, wearing the clothes of our new brothers.The elders of the tribe even gave the name of that winter's count as: "The-time-the mud-people-came-to-live-free-and-touch-the-sky."Marcus said grinning.

"Not long after that the elders decided we had proven ourselves.They gave Big John and me new names.Big John was called Strong Bear, and they called me Buffalo's Heart Long-bow."

Kah-La still needed to know one thing:"But how did you meet my mother?"He asked his father thru closed eyes. Marcus's memories flooded back to him. He smiled thoughtfully.

"Little-Pool-That-Shimmers was the sister of Chief Pallaton Bear Killer and Orenda Silver Wing and Onawa Blue Feather, Yawns-a-Lots' mother,"said Marcus fondly. He thought back to the time when their eyes first met.

"It was Little-Pool-That-Shimmers who chose me, said she liked me as soon as she saw me, even with all that dirt all over me.I wouldn't have picked her out as the prettiest woman, but she was gentle and kind and seemed to understand all I'd been through."Marcus tossed more twigs on the fire and leaned back again.

"It was strange spending time with her as a free man.I mean every day, Big John and I expected to be caught and hauled away by slavers or hung as murderers.I didn't think it was ever possible to be close to any woman, or ever laugh.It took a long while because I didn't know what to make of their ways, but your mother was going to get her way and then in no time at all she got the best of me and eventually became a part of me.She was a good woman.Your mother taught me so many things— about the land, about the animal spirits—She showed me real caring, my son."Marcus smiled.

"There is a saying between a man and woman when they give their hearts to one another.They exchange tokens of endearment and repeat: "May the stars and moon be a witness to my heart.My son, your mother was the very best part of me, a part of me that'll never be replaced,"said Marcus thoughtfully.

Kah-La thought for a moment and nodded. He tried to remember his mother's likeness.

"I don't see my mother's face in Orenda Silver Wing, for she is very old, but I see my mother's kind face in Onawa Blue Feather and in my sister, but I don't remember her that much, father."Kah-La said slowly. He shook his head.

"What happened to her, father?How did she die?"Kah-La asked intently."You must let me continue telling my story, my son,"Marcus said gently. A shadow of a smile crossed his face. But the telling of their family history would also bring an added burden Marcus knew would ultimately change him. He was tired but pleased his son wanted to know more about his mother.

"It was at one of our powwows—sometime after Big John and I came to live with the humans.I saw her dance and I never saw anything so beautiful—couldn't take my eyes off of her. Then we had your sister then you. And it was at a harvest festival, when we got word that soldiers were looking for runaway slaves. Big John had become a mountain man—a fur-trapper. He had taken several wives and felt that it was best he moved north—to Kanata to keep from getting captured. Your mother and I decided that we would stay with her family. Her father was an old man and refused to leave so we moved around following the herds. Then it got harder and harder because the iron road was being built. We had very little food left when the soldiers came."

"We could not grow our crops, our hunts were unsuccessful and one day your brave mother and some of the unmarried women had gone to the trading post in Clear Creek to trade blankets and bead-work. They were just about starved when they got there, and against their better judgment, they stayed on to eat a much needed meal before they headed back. Your mother had eaten with a metal utensil instead of a wooden one. And by the time they got back to the village, your mother was very weak and sick to her stomach. Do you remember?" Marcus asked.

"No, you wouldn't have, you were too young. The women kept you and your sister away so's you two wouldn't get sick too."

"It wasn't long and then she died. And then some of the elders started getting sick and they died off pretty quick too.Our medicine couldn't cure the white man's diseases.I knew she shouldn't have gone to the post—I had a bad feeling about it—but she insisted because we needed food and supplies.After that the women took care of you and your sister while the men hunted.Your aunts' Orenda Silver Wing and Onawa Blue Feather helped me raise you and your sister.So now you know all there is to tell, my son," Marcus said solemnly. "We must rest now my son, it is late."

That was two years ago Kah-La remembered. He shivered in the cold.

A Bad Decision

Kah-La wiped the stinging snow from his face. He thought of his father Marcus lying in his tipi back in the village. He'd been shot in the back by a soldier during an ambush at Butte Plains Pointe. Many braves had been killed that day. Opa Little Wing, the medicine woman was sitting with him day and night, praying over him, shaking her snake rattles to help ward off evil spirits. They would be burning sacred fires and giving him herbs and a watery soup broth to heal him till they returned with fresh meat.

Kah-La was determined to help his cousin Yawns-a-Lot get food to help their starving tribe. More than anything, he wanted his father to have a chance to survive the winter. Yawns-a-Lot, his 19 year old cousin, bit his wind-burned lips, hoping for movement soon. Their food was as scarce as the small bag of gunpowder and pellets they carried for the single musket rifle they carried with them. When they left on their journey, the tribal council made sure each hunter was supplied—each had a small pouch of dried meat and roots, some salt, dried fruits and nuts, a skin pouch with herbs and spices. But their rations were dwindling. The other hunters were lost. They needed fresh meat and a warm fire if they were to survive the deadly ordeal they now found themselves in—the boys were freezing to death.

The piercing cold and blustery wind brought one blessing—their enemies would not be out pursuing them in this weather. But they still had to keep a constant vigil just in case.

Crazy Bear, Hawk-Eye, He-who-Spits, Yawns-a-Lot and Kah-La were also given the best weapons for their hunt. Crazy Bear would lead them despite the warnings of the old shaman. The two young cousins had never been on a hunt without their fathers. Now they were alone and in dire circumstances.

Crazy Bear had become chief after his brother, Strong-Hands was killed a year before. He and his brother Strong-Hands had watched as their father; Red Cloud was shot from his horse at the Hollow. Then Strong-Hands, the father of Yawns-a-Lot, had become chief, only to be killed twelve moons ago with 40 other warriors in a massacre at Moose Creek.

A headstrong warrior, Crazy Bear had always competed to prove himself a courageous warrior. He had no problem taking leadership of the tribe. He was a member of the council, and now the keeper of the Rain Bundle, though he no longer took its sacred powers seriously. Strong-Hands had always told the council that his brother Crazy Bear would not make a good leader. But since he was now the keeper of the Rain-Bundle, the Elders had felt Crazy Bear was their best choice—He was youthful.

Crazy Bear refused to carry the Rain-Bundle with them to the hunt; he said it was superstitious nonsense. His young nephew Yawns-a-Lot knew better. In a dream he had the night before they were to leave for the hunt, the Great Good Spirit told him that the Sacred Rain Bundle would protect him on the hunt. And as the five-member hunting party headed north to the high country to find the game they desperately needed, Yawns-a-Lot knew they'd have to count on Crazy Bear's leadership—although he wouldn't depend on it. He would be carrying Sacred Rain Bundle.

On the second morning of the hunt, Kah-La and Yawns-a-Lot dismounted and were unpacking the ponies to set up camp. Crazy Bear and Hawk-Eye and He-who-Spits, had stepped away from camp to the edge of a small ravine to make water. Kah-La spotted a dead branch ideal for firewood, and had just picked it up when he caught the sight of a weasels running out of, instead of into, a hole in the ground. Suddenly a flock of birds scattered into the air. Then he heard the panicked hoof beats of their spooked ponies and felt the ground shake. He grabbed a tree and hung on for dear life, which is where Yawns-a-Lot found him.

The violent earthquake left a crack in the earth wide enough for several large animals to fall thru. And they followed it. The disturbed earth had collapsed in on itself and had sealed itself up swallowing the men. Nearby they had found a few scattered supplies—a cooking pot and a few wooden bowls and spoons in a skin pouch. They found several warriors' rations, the tipi, and a quiver of arrows, a peace pipe and a few bed rolls. They found several broken arrows—a bad omen. The two boys put their ears to the ground. They heard no other signs of life.

"Oo—ee—la!"Yawns-a-Lot called. He called again."Oo—ee—la!"Silence. They knew.

Kah-La looked to his cousin, too stunned to say anything. All he could think of was old Tokala Fire Eyes' dream. In their hearts the boys knew their fellow hunters had perished within the earth. New Chief Crazy Bear should have heeded the warnings of the old medicine man.

The boys collected their scant supplies and placed them in a pile. With the ponies gone, it would be impossible to carry a great deal. They separated the skins of the tipi so they could bundle and carry what they could. Now the village's survival was on their shoulders—though, back in the village, no one yet knew.

At training to become a warrior, all young lads were instructed in the skill of survival. Before birth; mothers would prepare their sons for endurance as warriors by making spiritual amulets to wear around their necks to protect them. Whether they would become warriors, hunters, shamans, or scouts, fathers would give their sons toy-sized weapons to play with. And as soon as a boy could stand, he was given a bow.

The community held races to see who could swim and run the fastest. They learned to track animals and their enemies. They learned how to find water and how to shoot their arrows from any position, even while riding a horse. And when an older male child is ready they embark on a vision quest— usually alone. It's a rite of passage taken at a turning point in life; before puberty to find oneself—for spiritual and life direction. But for Yawns-a-Lot and Kah-La this wasn't a vision quest—this was different—it was worse.

The boy's had been trained how to listen to the winds for the approach of game, how to shoot an arrow and throw a spear, how to skin an animal and prepare the meat for the smoking racks. They knew the Great Good Spirit was with them but their outcome appeared as dismal as the bitter winter before them.

Kah-La relaxed his arms. He could almost hear his mother's—Little Pool-That-Shimmers'—voice from the spirit world: "Be brave, Kah-La, my son. You can do this."

No one would be coming to rescue them. They were alone in an ice-covered and bleak wilderness, having to depend solely on one another. They had no idea how long it would take them to get back to the camp—or if they would.

How many days would it take to get back to the village on foot?How would they be able to carry game back—that is, if they could find any with their limited ammunition and energy?Would they survive? Or would their frozen bodies be found in the spring thaw?

A Bird in the Hand

Snow began to fall—lightly at first. The boys'
hollow bellies were filled with the cold. They were
shivering. Kah-La's arms ached from holding the
bow and arrow against his shoulder. Bracing
himself, he lowered his arms and adjusted the
Buffalo skin robe that covered his head. He took a
deep breath and closed his eyes while his cousin kept
watch. He tugged on his talisman around his neck.
Then quickly drifted off and dreamt of fires burning
brightly in the center of a large room. He could smell
the meat and vegetables being cooked with herbs
from his aunt's garden and could see the steam rise
from the clay pot. How delicious it would taste!He
dreamt he was snuggled beneath the warm animal
robes in the lodge and watching their happy lives
unfold—

Kah-La's brief nap was shattered. He'd been
awakened by the sharp crack of musket fire.

"Oo—ee—la."Yawns-a-Lot whooped."Oo—ee—
la."He yelled again.

Kah-La stood and watched as his cousin leaped
through the heavy snowdrifts to collect the bird he'd
shot. He was grinning—satisfied as he brought it
back to where Kah-La stood. With his knife Yawns-
a-Lot quickly cut out the heart of the bird and
handed it to the younger boy. He ate some of the

warm innards, and then let Kah-La sip some of its blood so he could stay warmer a bit longer.

Their people believed that if they ate the heart of their kill, they could become one with its spirit. Both boys thanked the Great Good Spirit for sending them fresh meat. Yawns-a-Lot plucked the pellet from the bird and wiped it off. He tucked it back into the beaded bag along with the others; and cleaned his knife in the snow and re sheathed it. He breathed in the sweet crisp, cold air and wrapped the bird carefully. They would have to move on to find a safe shelter so they could properly roast their kill.

"We'll go to the cave at Eagle's Peak,"Yawns-a-Lot said. That is if there is no animal already in it. He thought to himself. Kah-La said nothing. It was still early morning. The boys pulled together their belongings and shaking the snow from the tipi, they and secured them. Steadying himself with the butt of the rifle, Yawns-a-Lot stood with his bundle and squinted. He nodded to Kah-La and headed in the direction of the trees dotting the edge of the field. The tops of the trees caught the new snow. They would make their own path, trudging beneath the trees where the snow-fall was thinnest.

So far the two young warriors had been fortunate— they were still alive. And by what light they still had they would use it to cover a lot of ground. It would be unfortunate for them if the bird's bloody scent was carried on the wings of the wind. The falling

snow would however deter their two-legged
enemies—or so they hoped.

"Oo—ee—la, Oo—ee—la,"Yawns-a-Lot screeched
at the top of his lungs, the hot mist rising from his
breath like tendrils of smoke in the frozen air.

"Oo—ee—la,"he hollered again; straining to voice a
courage he didn't own.

The boys continued to trudge beneath the trees along
the creek. The heavy snow slowed the young braves
down. Once in a while they'd stop to shift their
bundles and adjust their robes. The raw meat lay
heavy in their stomachs. Undaunted; they continued
their slow pace. Kah-La still had not spoken. Anger
and fear had locked his tongue. His people trusted
the Great Good Spirit, but they also knew Coyote
would be on their heels. The earth swallowed their
kinsmen?—he wanted to scream at the top of his
young lungs. Crazy Bear should have heeded Old
Tokala Fire Eyes' warning.

Yawns-a-Lot was angry too—at Crazy Bear for
leading them into misfortune and himself for letting
himself be led? But at least they were alive. Coyote
must be smiling now that they were stranded and
alone.

The cousins briefly made eye contact for the first
time since they'd been alone. Yawns-a-Lot
understood his cousin's distress but showed little

emotion. Kah-La couldn't speak. He was afraid that if he did, he would cry like a baby. Yawns-a-Lot, lost in his own thoughts—of the friends they'd lost—killed in the many battles with their enemies—pushed down the grief that kept rising up. Both boys held a secret hope that somehow their ponies would return to them.

Slowly they continued to maneuver thru and beneath the outline of trees. Stopping now and again to rest and readjust the awkward bundles they carried. But then they sensed something—A low throaty moan could be heard just above the scream of the wind. Uneasiness crept into the minds of both boys. The two quickened their pace. They heard it again—louder now. They could not see the beast, but they knew how it moved and they sensed where it was. The animal was hungry. The scent of their kill drew the animal. And it smelled their fear and was stalking them.

Yawns-a-Lot probed the ground with the butt of his musket rifle. He wanted more than the bone knife he carried, to protect them; he needed a sharp spear. As both boys prodded through the snow with their awkward bundles, Yawns-a-Lot noticed the outline of a sturdy branches poking thru the snow. Removing his mittens he snapped off a piece of oneand passed the musket to his young cousin. Without breaking stride he began to whittle away. The implement was taking shape as they pressed thru the soft snowdrifts. With one end sharpened Yawns-a-Lot switched it around and sharpened the other end while Kah-La kept in step. Both boys scanned their surroundings for the prowling animal but saw nothing but shadows.

"Oo—ee—la—Oo—ee—la." Yawns-a-Lot screeched; to caution the animal not to come any closer. Their hearts pounded rapidly as they trudged onward thru the heavy snow drifts.

Moving in tandem; the snow crunched beneath their feet. Kah-La's foot found another limb poking up from the snow. He shifted the pack on his back and retrieved it. They thanked the Great Good Spirit for their find. Yawns-a-Lot exchanged the finished weapon for the stick that Kah-La found. Again he whittled until they had two crudely sharpened walking stick/spears for protection. The boys trudged at a faster pace now, plowing through shifting drifts and falling snow. They were warmer—almost sweating, but that too was a risk. They could not take a chance of sweating in the freezing cold without a place to dry off. They could not afford to panic.

The animal keened and kept pace with them. They paused and adjusted their awkward belongings yet again—pulling their skins snuggly about them. They lowered their faces against the stinging cold and used their spears and musket to steady themselves. Fear kept them awake and alive. All day they walked at a steady pace stopping to rest briefly. The bird was wrapped securely so no animal could detect it. It had been rolled in snow and secured in skins.

Eagles Peak: The Cave

It was dark when they at last got to the base of
Eagles Peak, where they stopped to shift the weight
of their packs again to prepare for their ascent up the
snowy terrain. Weariness had overcome them, but
fear kept them moving. Both boys knew that if the
cave wasn't empty—it was most likely an animal's
den. They used the sharpened sticks to move through
the brush and frozen snow, maneuvering past gopher
holes, loose rocks and branches. It was late evening
when they reached their final destination; a low-
slung rock overhang behind a row of brush. Yawns-
a-Lot had been there several times before after a
hunt.

This time he was praying to the Great Good Spirit—
hoping there wasn't animals already hiding in the
cave for the winter. They squinted and tried peer into
the dark cavernous space. The opening narrowed. It
was too dark to see anything. They held their spears
out in front of them and held their breath. They
listened. All they could hear was an echo of the
howling wind bouncing off the stone walls inside the
cave. They set down their bundles. Kah-La stood
with his bow and arrow at the ready. Yawns-a-Lot
removed his mittens and knelt at the entrance
groping the underbrush for drier kindling. Blocking
the wind with their bodies, Yawns-a-Lot struck his
precious flint with trembling hands—trying to coax a
flame. Both boys were willing the fire to ignite.
Would the kindling they found be dry enough?

Yawns-a-Lot struck the flint again and again, both boys, keeping cautious eyes toward the back of the cave. Still there was no flame. There was no sound stirring from the cave either. Yawn's-a-Lot's hands were too cold—His fingers too numb. But they could not give up.

Kah-La knew he would have to try something different. He aimed and let several arrows fly from his bow into the caves entrance. Straining above the howling wind, they listened—nothing. Kah-La exchanged his bow and arrow for his spear and knife and waded into the dark musty cavern. Moments later he returned with a handful of dried pine needles and leaves and set them in a small pile in front of his cousin. Once more he struck the flint to kindling, and struck again. Finally a tiny blue blaze burst forth from the dried needles with a sizzle. Kah-La added more leaves—careful to not let the fire smother. His eyes darted about the cave. Indeed, they seemed to be the only occupants. The boys cautiously removed their robes, shook the snow from them and donned them again. They kept their eyes on the shadows of the darkened cave. No sounds. Kah-La picked up a flaming stick from the fire and raised it above his head.

The cave was small but large enough to see they were alone. Faded paintings of animals and village life of an ancient people covered the walls. Yawns-a-Lot took sticks to move the fire to the inside of the cave. Once the fire was going, he spread out the tipi to dry and spread out their belongings. Yawn's-a-Lot joined Kah-La. On the walls and ceiling of the small cave Yawns-a-Lot recognized the markings, and remembered the stories he had heard when he'd been there before. The boys found more remnants of shards of pottery and branches and dried grasses that others had left in the cave. Along the floor of one wall they found animal dung, dried moss and sticks—a gift from the Great Good Spirit, who seemed to be answering their prayers of gratitude in the whistling winds. They gathered up armfuls of sticks and set them beside the fire. Then they scrounged along the entrance of the cave for more pine needles to dry and use later.

The boys, still chilly from the cold; breathed in the smoky damp odor of pine needles from the small crackling fire. From where they stood no one could see the fire which blazed near the entrance to the cave. They set out supplies to roast the bird. They were almost too cold and tired to prepare their meager meal. Yawns-a-Lot un-wrapped the bird and Kah-La gathered snow into a wooden bowl and set it beside the fire to melt. They placed the bird in it so its skin could loosen the feathers making it easier to pluck. The feeling in their numbed fingers and toes were slowly returning. The boys worked in tandem and in silence.

Yawns-a-Lot donned his buffalo robe and stepped outside the cave to find more sticks and vines along the entrance and listened for the animal that had been stalking them. They broke down the sticks with their mocassined boots and whittled the sticks into sharp points making several dozen of them.

Yawns-a-Lot shoved the sharpened sticks into the frozen ground at the entrance of their temporary dwelling. Kah-La returned to the fire, removed his moccasins, setting them in front of the fire to dry along with his mittens. Then he began plucking the bird. Covered and hidden with twigs and leaves, several rows of sharpened tips, crisscrossed the entrance to the cave. Yawns-a-Lot remove a small piece of dried jerky and set it in his jaw. He held a piece out to his young cousin, but Kah-La shook his head and kept working; rubbing herbs and salting the bird. They heard the same piercing growl over the wind. Perhaps it smelled their fear, it would however soon smell their food. Kah-La handed off the readied bird to Yawns-a-Lot to roast then he retired to the pallet by the fire and was fast asleep.

Remembering

Yawns-a-Lot pierced the skin of the bird with a sharpened stick and propped it over the fire to roast. He recalled an image from his childhood—the contorted face and body of Sho-Su-Na; another cousin, who had almost died after being mauled by a bear. It too was in winter. A small hunting party had been stalking the animal but had only wounded it. Sho-Su-Na teased the animal but was too close. Enraged, the great beast lunged and took a swipe at his head with his enormous paws; flipping the young warrior into the air. But before they could kill the animal it lunged and sunk its teeth into the boys' shoulder, almost tearing him apart. The bear was finally killed by the hunting party before it could kill the lad. Yawn's-a-Lot shuddered.

Sho-Su-Na was horribly disfigured and had lost an eye but the boy lived. He was nursed back to health by Opa-Little-Wing, who was now keeper of the medicine bundle of their dwindling clan. The previous medicine man, White-Running Deer had been her husband but had been killed in battle. Ordinarily medicine men were not part of the fray, keeping a safe distance away—with faces painted, they chanted prayers of protection, shaking their medicine bags and spears high over their heads while battles erupted before them. But White-Running Deer had gotten too close…taking a bullet released by a man from the army of the long knives. Opa Little Wing was stronger and wiser than most of the

men in the village and had continued her husband's
role as keeper of the village's medicine bundle and
she relied on the visions of the old shaman; Tokala
Fire Eyes.

The Cave

Yawn's-a-Lot brought his thoughts back to the present when the skin of the bird sizzled. He turned it around to roast on the other side. He stared into the flames, stirred and added more kindling to the burning coals. They were safe for now. Outside, the ceaseless wind whipped savagely. It's haunting and ghostly noise echoing off the walls of the cave. Yawn's-a-Lot drew his robes around him and stood. He stepped to the mouth of the cave again to look out while his young cousin slept. Snow clouds were blotting out the stars.

The night was black. Yawns-a-Lot cleaned his hands in the snow, dried them on his leggings, and went to his bedroll to remove the sacred object he had hidden there. He took out the Rain-Bundle from his bedroll and examined it. When he looked up Kah-La was watching him. He held it up showing it to Kah-La for the first time. Startled; Kah-La sat up and looked at the Rain Bundle in stunned silence. Each boy knew they shouldn't be handling something so sacred without prayers of protection, but it had protected them. Kah-La looked at his cousin for a long time in disbelief then he lay back on his pallet and closed his eyes again. Yawns-a-Lot reverently returned the Rain-Bundle to his bedroll without explanation. He sharpened his bone knife on a smooth rock and went to gather more kindling by leaning over the sharpened sticks at the entrance to the cave. He filled several of the bowls with ice to melt by the heat of the fire. Outside in the distance he heard it—the now-familiar growl. The predator smelled their kill—roasting.

Missing Home

As Yawns-a-Lot sat reminiscing about his old life, Kah-La had curled up once more and was fast asleep. He slept and dreamt of the happy gathering of the yearly Green Corn Festival; which lasted several days. He dreamt he was helping the women pour the maize onto his mother's grinding stone. Little-Pool-That-Shimmers and the other women of their clan was grinding grain into meal to make bread. The children played and were tossing spears thru hoops. Others rode their ponies in a race. Laughter and drumbeats echoed thru their community.

"Oo—ee—la." He heard the children yell. "Oo—ee—la." The children were happy. They whooped and danced when Kras-N-Nah climbed the great tree to reach the honey comb. The older boy cut the comb down and tossed it to the shouting children below. The laughing children ran from the angry bees. Everyone broke off pieces of the honeycomb as they dodged the stinging swarm. They sampled the sweet oozing nectar and licked it off their fingers and kept running back to sample more. The day was perfect—except it was only a dream.

Kah-La breathed in the scent of roasting meat. He had dreamt of food: it tugged at his stomach. He untangled himself from his robes—starved. Kah-La rubbed his eyes and sat up completely. Immediately the boy was overcome with a deep sorrow when he realized where he was not. And his body ached. The wind continued to howl outside. Yawn's-a-Lot hadn't fallen asleep. He sat wrapped in his robes tending the fire which was heating the cave and drying their wet belongings. Kah-La pulled his robe about him and moved closer to the fire. Silently the two watched the flickering firelight make odd shadows on the walls of the cave. The meat was ready.

The tantalizing smell of roasting meat mingled with musty air, overcoming it. The boys had done well to meet the challenge they faced so far, but their challenges were far from over. They still needed meat for the village to survive. Perhaps they could use the cave as a base till they found food. But the pained expression on the Kah-La's face mirrored Yawn's-a-Lot's—who was also haunted by the last sight of the hunting party. There was nothing the boys could have done. Crazy Bear should have listened to the old Shaman; Tokala Fire Eyes.

Yawns-a-Lot scrubbed off a large flat rock with dried vines and melted snow so that the meat could be evenly divided. The two cousins offered up prayers of thanks to the Great Good Spirit for their shelter and food. They ate slowly, chewing carefully, spitting any stray un-plucked feathers into the fire. A tear ran down Kah-La's cheek and he angrily brushed it away with his fist.

They threw the bones into the fire and added more kindling to bank the fire for the night. They sharpened their knives. Again a tear ran down Kah-La's face, but he turned away. He would not allow his cousin to see his weakness. Yawns-a-Lot sated his thirst then handed the water-skin to Kah-La. The younger boy drank from it and returned the skin. He lingered by the entrance to clean the wooden bowl. He filled it with more snow, carefully stepping back over the sharpened sticks. The bowl was placed by the fire. He retired to his pallet; covered himself with his Buffalo robe and wept silently into them.

Wrapped in his robe, Yawns-a-Lot rolled onto his side and stared into the fire. He remembered the many evenings with the older warriors, the voices of their fathers and uncles, listening to their stories of raids and hunts while the peace pipe was passed around. Stories exchanged of shaming their enemies by counting coups—touching them and taking their ponies and weapons. There would be no more gathering of these same warriors—many of them were gone. He closed his eyes inviting sleep come.

Yawns-a-Lot's Confidence

He had to encourage the boy to survive to continue. He hadn't shown weakness. He decided it was time for Kah-La to earn his talisman. The boy had never been on a vision quest and this was as much of a vision quest as he was going to get. Yawns-a-Lot recalled the boy's courageous act of going into the cave without any idea what was there.He smiled— yawning. He stretched himself. Relaxing his tense muscles for the first time in days—He wrestled with what they would to do about their present dilemma. Tomorrow would be another day—another very cold day.

Kah-La had endured much—they both had in fact. But Yawns-a-Lot considered the young lads strength. He barely made a sound when the ground trembled—still hadn't. But he had not broken. He did not cry out as children do when they're hurt or wail as women often do when they lose their husbands in battle. Yawns-a-Lot thought about their families. And now he had to process the loss of the hunting party and as Kah-La would have to do in his own way. The boy had shown true strength by saying nothing. Yawns-a-Lot was certain that with a new name, the boy would become a strong warrior some day and for that he was very proud.

The Lion and Kah-La's Weapon

"Oo—ee—la;" yelled Yawns-a-Lot. It was light.
Kah-La awakened with a start. His body ached. He
needed to make water. He rubbed his eyes and
looked about the dimly lit cave. More sticks had
been added to the fire. "Oo—ee—la" Yawns-a-Lot
yelled again; from outside. "Oo—ee—la". Kah-La
answered from inside the cave.

Kah-La heard the unexpected shrill and desperate
call of a loon—a signal that something was terribly
wrong; Kah-La ran to the mouth of the cave and
looked out. It had stopped snowing. The brilliant sun
glistened off the snowy landscape blinding him.
Again Kah-La heard the call of the loon.

"Oo—ee—la". His cousin—his brother was in
trouble and needed his help. Kah-La noticed that
Yawns-a-Lot had removed some of the stakes at his
feet and leaned out even further to see. Yawns-a-Lot
was on his back. He had fallen into a gopher hole
and twisted his ankle. Kah-La was unaware the
crouching mountain lion above him. He grabbed the
weapon he'd prepared during the night and made his
way down the steep embankment. Yawns-a-Lot
cried out. And in the blink of an eye the heavy beast
roared and leaped.

Sensing a shadow above him, Kah-La took a deep
breath and steadied himself with both hands. He
clutched the spear and turned and thrust it forward.

The huge cat landed atop of him. Blood sprayed across the snowy hillside while Yawns-a-Lot watched in horror. His helpless cousin tumbled end over end down the embankment; entangled in the body of the deadly beast. With his heart in his throat and his knife in hand, the terrified teen ignored the throbbing pain in his ankle and lunged after them. He was savagely determined to kill the beast and rescue his cousin from its clutches. When he reached the bottom of the hill, he threw himself on the beast—at its throat. His heart clubbing his ribs. For a brief moment the animal writhed in pain one last time but then was lying still—dead. He thanked the Great Good Spirit.

Yawns-a-Lot noticed the spear that had snapped off and was sticking out of the animal's chest. Kah-La rolled away, un-harmed except for a few minor scrapes. He jumped up quickly, completely covered in blood—seemingly unaffected by what had just taken place."I have to make water,"the boy said before running off.Yawns-a-Lot tried to stand, but sat down hard from the pain. He examined his swollen ankle and thanked the Great Good Spirit again for keeping Kah-La from being killed.

Kah-La showed great bravery. But what now? Yawns-a-Lot knew they couldn't hunt the way he was now. He was in a great deal of pain and could not walk. How would they survive? Were the spirits mocking him? Was Coyote laughing at them? He couldn't make it back to their people on foot—not without some time to heal. And certainly not without the meat that was promised. They would need to skin the lion and cure the meat first; he reasoned.

Then Yawns-a-Lot looked closely at the broken spear sticking out of the dead lioness and was surprised to see the boy's handy-work. It was not one spear but two. Kah-La had taken strips of dried vines, tying and knotting them tightly together at the top the middle and bottom; making it one weapon. He even managed to use his own medicine bag for the bottom to hold the spear together. Kah-La had wet the bag and wrapped it with strips of buffalo skin and let it dry tight by the fire during the night.

"Ah, he was not sleeping,"said Yawns-a-Lot; aloud."The boy stood firm like a Buffalo and is a worthy warrior. His father would be proud. He is truly a warrior now."Yawns-a-Lot whispered to the winds around him. Because of the boy, the animal was dead and they were both still alive.

"Kah-La must have a new name. I will call him: Buffalo-Stands-Firm."He will no longer be teased and made fun of—at least not by him.

But where was Kah-La? He wondered. He should have returned by now. He would need his help to get back up to the cave. And they would have to do something about the lions' carcass.Yawns-a-Lot was not looking forward to the task of skinning the animal, which would likely bring more danger to them from animals seeking food.

Yawns-a-Lot heard movement—riders on Fback; moving thru the snowdrifts but he could not see from his vantage-point. He pulled out his knife; knowing that he was at a disadvantage. Whoever was coming would have already seen the bloody path down the hill; had Kah-La been captured by their enemies? He wondered.

"Oo—ee—la."Kah-La called to him. Yawns-a-Lot hesitated to call back. Someone was with him. Was the wind deceiving him? Was it coyotes' foolishness? He imagined?

"Oo—ee—la."Kah-La called again. It was him! Yawns-a-Lot called back and the ten year old appeared, mounted on his own pony. Not only that, he was leading four warriors, along with their ponies that had escaped the earthquake. Yawns-a-Lot saw his pony and whistled. The pony ran to him and nuzzled his shoulder. His heart leaped. The animal had been fed. Yawns-a-Lot wrapped a hand in the pony's mane and pulled himself up and tried awkwardly to stand. He winced and eyed the warriors suspiciously—it was apparent they had food.

The traveling warriors; using words and signs they knew in common, explained that they had been to Eagle Rock Falls, near the ravine where the ground had opened up and swallowed the hunters. They too had felt the earth tremble and had seen where the ground had opened and closed. The ponies had run as far as White Willow Peak, where the warriors had found them and rounded them up. They'd followed the horse tracks back to the site of the disturbance. Then they'd followed the boys' footprints in the snow to the cave. From the markings on the warriors' ponies and clothing, Yawns-a-Lot recognized them as allies. They exchanged greetings and introduced themselves.

Grey Bear, Lean Wolf, Little Turtle and Sky Hawk were returning from a raid and had extended the unusual kindness of returning their ponies.In a dialect similar to their own, Lean Wolf told Yawns-a-Lot, "You have done well." He nodded toward the slain beast lying in a heap on the ground. The men with him nodded, too—impressed.

Yawns-a-Lot shook his head,"It was not my doing."He nodded toward Kah-La, who had jumped down from his pony. Kah-La walked over to the lion's body and kicked it, the broken spear still sticking out of its bloodied chest. Kah-La raised his chin and Yawns-a-Lot laid a hand on his shoulder."I will now call you Buffalo-Stands-Firm,"he said.The boy looked surprised, but kept silent.

He turned to face the warriors "It was my cousin, Buffalo-Stands-Firm,"Yawns-a-Lot said proudly; trying out the new name. He grinned at his young cousin. The men looked on, surprised and amused but impressed.

Allies

The four warriors made a clearing in the snow and unloaded their supplies from their ponies. They set up a large tipi, and built a fire to cook several rabbits and a few fish they had caught earlier. They made a small fire and turned back the flap of the tipi for ventilation. They gave the boys some dried strips of venison to eat in the meantime. They passed around a peace pipe while the meat was cooking and they shared their stories. The boys listened but were still a little cautious. Grey Bear, Lean Wolf, Little Turtle and Sky Hawk agreed to help the boys hunt and bring back food to the village.

"Buffalo-Stands-Firm?" Little Turtle asked then pointed to the dead lioness. "What do you intend to do with your first kill?"

Kah-La still felt shy about speaking. He did nothing to deny or admit to his new name. He looked at his cousin and made motions toward the carcass. "He wants to skin it and share it with you," Yawns-a-Lot told the men.

The four warriors looked at each other and tried to keep from smiling. No one wanted to tell Kah-La that the lioness' powerful muscles would make tough meat. What could they say? The boy had shown courage and performed a remarkable feat well beyond his young age. At last the corners of the boy's mouth turned—a little.

The men helped to hang the carcass from a nearby tree while Yawns-a-Lot sat watching them. They helped to steady the animal while Kah-La made the first cut, down the middle of the animal's chest. He tugged and pulled the knife with all his might as he had watched the men of his village do. The men showed him how to quarter and salt the meat and cut thin strips to smoke over the fire. He would keep the lion's teeth and take them back to his father.

After the ponies were watered and fed, Gray Bear and Lean Wolf motioned for the newly named Buffalo-Stands-Firm to keep an eye on the curing meat. They had assembled sticks to set Yawns-a-Lot's leg. Then they climbed the hill headed for the cave. Little Turtle helped Yawns-a-Lot and led the procession up a narrow, hidden path that snaked up the hill. The warriors knew the cave. Once inside Yawns-a-Lot hobbled to his beading and wrapped himself in his robe: shivering. He watched as Little Turtle and Sky Hawk removed skins they had brought with them, eachdumping something out of them toward the back of the cave. While lean Wolf and Grey Bear removed the stakes at the entrance they rekindled the smoldering coals and made a fire. Among their belongings they pulled out a peace pipe and some tobacco, warming themselves while Yawns-a-Lot watched.

Back at the campfire at the bottom of the hill Kah-La was getting restless and bored. He didn't dwell on what had happened earlier but was curious as to what was taking place in the cave. The Great Good spirit had protected them once again. But it started to snow again. At first he pretended to be diligent in his meat-smoking tasks.He was not frightened. He removed the most cured strips of meat and flipped them. He removed the driest pieces of smoked meat from the bottom rack and then flipped them over onto the tallest part of the smoking rack; away from the heat. He wondered why he wasn't included with the men and his cousin, but he kept to his task.

The warriors finally returned at dark bringing wood. They put blankets over the ponies' backs and sat by the fire in the tipi. Sky Hawk gave Buffalo-Stands-Firm a pouch to store the prepared lion's meat. The young hunter said nothing. He just grinned and passed the pouch around. Each man took a slim piece of the salted meat.

As they chewed the tough meat, the warriors told stories. Lean Wolf told how the Cheyenne nation had migrated onto the planes along the Missouri River in South Dakota, and how they prospered and grew. And as woodland people, they had been preyed upon for decades by other tribes and nearly wiped out. Everything changed when their ancestors were able to round up and capture ponies. Through test after test they became skilled horsemen, formidable fighters and expert buffalo hunters. Then they shared stories about competing with their former enemies.

Sky Hawk's father's tribe, a different group, had adopted the custom of packing tipis and taking their families in pursuit of the buffalo herds.

"We may not see buffalo tomorrow,"he said. "But I know where the deer often hide in winter. We will go to that place."He said between bites of food.

As the wind screamed and the fire whipped and blazed, the boys dozed off listening to the warriors' stories of buffalo hunts and raids on the white settlers.

During the night, Buffalo-Stands-Firm was awakened by a far-off growl: the moan of a lion that had lost his mate. He thought of the women in his village that would learn, in a few days that they were widows.

Young Warriors Homecoming

Yawns-a-Lot and Buffalo-Stands-Firm rode their ponies just ahead of their new allies. "Oo—ee—la.Oo—ee—la."They called as they rode in arms raised high—a friendly signal to the village scouts who they knew would be watching. Slung on the backs of the pack ponies were the carcasses of 2 deer, and the pelt of one mountain lion.

It was late when they arrived. The news of the hunting party's arrival spread quickly throughout the village. Only the two youngest warriors had returned from the hunt—and they had brought with them visitors. Widows learning of their husband's demise rent their clothes and cut their hair.

The people in the village worked quickly to help unpack the ponies. But there would be meat for a feast that night.

An old woman directed the visitors to the men's tipi and gave them skin rags to wash with. Someone else handed them several wooden bowls of soup. The Elders called a meeting. Old Tokala Fire Eyes; the medicine man, was assisted to the lodge. And what had once been a male-only meeting was now being witnessed by the women too. They waited for the two youngest warriors, who would sit in council and tell their story first.

Upon arrival, Kah-La had slipped away to visit his father's tipi. He shook the flap of the tent; saw his aunt Onawa-Blue Feather's smile. She was stirring her clay pot of corn soup over a welcoming fire. Opa Little Wing, the medicine woman, sat at the foot of the bed, chanting and praying softly, her drum; singing a healing song. Nearby Satinka Doe Foot sat chanting with her drum. Marcus, surrounded in blankets and furs, his midsection bandaged, struggled to sit up and greet his son.

Kah-La stood before his father, taller than when he had left. Dressed in tattered moccasins, he had outgrown his leggings and breechcloth.

"Kah-La?"Marcus whispered, squinting in the dim light. He had spent the entire time they were away; praying to the God of his grandmother; for their safe return.

Kah-La dropped to his knees, his eyes filling with the tears he was unable to shed before. Marcus touched his son's face. "My son, it is good to set these eyes upon you."

"And you, father,"the boy finally spoke; his voice raw. Opa Little Wing and Satinka Doe Foot drummed and chanted louder.

"The council?"Marcus asked. He did not want his son to be late.

"I'll go with you."Onawa Blue Feather said as she stirred the large iron cauldron of corn soup and ladled it into a wooden bowl and handed the steaming soup to the boy. Kah-La knew she wanted to see her own son. He ate quickly. Onawa Blue Feather observed her nephew's sure footed gait—no longer a child's, but that of a proud young warrior who'd passed through a grown man's trials. She touched his arm briefly and left him at the men's tipi. but She would have to wait until after council to see her son, Yawns-a-Lot. Kah-La entered, strode to the circle and took his seat cross-legged on the floor, next to Yawn's-a-Lot. Still unready to speak; he nodded to older boy to begin.

Yawns-a-Lot carefully told their story. How he had brought along the mighty Rain Bundle to protect them when Crazy Bear refused. How the earth had opened and swallowed the three hunters. How the ponies had run off and how they had spent the night in the cave protecting themselves from the wind and the animals and how Buffalo-Stands-Firm got his new name by saving both their lives when he had killed the pouncing lioness.

Keening wails of grief and distress were heard from the women's tent, where several older women had gone to console the widows. Others in the community had begun tounpack and feed the ponies. All joined in and began skinning and butchering and treating the meat. They cut up chunks of meat and added to the pot of stew. The rest of the day would be spent curing leather and smoking meat well into the night and following morning. And finally, it was the visiting warriors' turn to tell their story—how they had found the ponies and eventually located the boys.

Council members passed the peace pipe. Its gray smoke rose, curling above their heads and out through the smoke hole of the tipi. As they finished their story, women and youngsters were bringing in wooden planks laden with bowls of soup—the hospitality of a grateful village.

The villagers discovered that one of the visitors, Gray Bear, was of a clan who had been split off from their own tribe. They were distant kinfolk, even though the markings of their ponies and their buffalo skins were different.

After the sharing of stories and food the council made a decision on when they would try to retrieve the bodies of the warriors from the ravine to bring them back to be properly mourned. Gray Bear brought a request to the council. The four visiting warriors expressed interest in marrying the women of childbearing age who had been left with no husbands. They needed the women's help to provide clothes and moccasins, to prepare food and to help raise children to keep the clan strong.

The recent widows of the village, which included Onawa Blue Feather and now the three wives of

Crazy Bear, wouldn't have to respond right away. It was understood that a year would be sufficient in their wait to marry. Two moons would pass before they could come back to attend another council. The women could then choose whether or not they wanted to accompany the warriors to the upcoming ceremonies. But now was too soon. The widows would need to mourn for their husbands by wailing and painting their faces and tearing their clothes.

After leaving the visitors in the men's tipi, some of the women of the clan fussed over the boys return, forcing a variety of herbal concoctions down their throats; especially Onawa Blue Feather; Yawns-a-Lot's mother. Yawns-a-Lot protested. He was a brave, a warrior and did not want to be seen as weak. Kah-La protested as well, putting up a good fight and then at long last giving in to the warmth of the women's mothering.

In the end the two were greeted warmly by Yawns-a-Lot mother; Onawa Blue Feather and Kah-La's sister; Tawa Morning Dance.

Over the next few days, the tribe would continue to share their stories. The dead warriors would be inducted into the Ghost Lodge. And almost too soon, the young warriors would have to step in and take their rightful places.

Well after the council meeting and mandatory care by the women of the village, Kah-La returned to his father's tipi, proudly carrying a small bundle. He sat down cross-legged beside his father's pallet and presented it: the pouch of dried lion meat, the lion's pelt, and his medicine bag full of lion's teeth.

"I hear you have a new name, my brave son."Marcus said. Kah-La looked more self-assured—he had grown several inches.

"What do you think of it my son?"Marcus asked curious. Kah-La grinned. He would have to speak the name out loud; to claim it for himself.

Kah-La shrugged."It was given to me by Yawns-a-Lot, Father." Marcus was proud of his son. He was proud of them both.

With a bashful grin, he removed the teeth of the lion from his medicine bag and held them out to his father. Marcus's eyes filled as his son finally told his story: It was a story the tribe would retell, among the stories of the battles. Kah-La; who would turn 11 in the next few days, was the youngest warrior the tribe ever had. Never again would he have to put up with the children's teasing about his woolly hair or full nose. Indeed, he would formally be given his name; Buffalo-Stands-Firm, who had killed the mountain lion—that is if he accepted the name given him by his cousin. Yawns-A-Lot had wisely taken the rain bundle and now it was his responsibility to care for what had protected them. Soon the four warriors were gone; leaving the encampment to visit with other clans' communities who were now being sought after by the armies of the long knives. The village would have to move further north; to higher ground.

The Warriors Ceremony

The following year; the day of the young warrior's ceremony was held at the Green Corn Festival. The women got up early to prepare the flat bread, the smoked and roasted meats, the dried pumpkin, squash and dried fruit, berries and nuts and deer stew with dried vegetables for the feast. They thanked the Great Good Spirit for their bounty. They blessed the earth and the animals.

Satinka Doe Foot had built an altar of white ash sticks for the Great Calumet—an offering. She was adorned and was wearing a heavy beaded buck-skin tunic with her hair pulled back. The drums began to beat softly. Everyone dressed in their treasured plumes began to chant. Marcus was able to walk with help to the ceremony.

Tokala Fire Eyes, the old medicine man, his body revealing naught of his age, stood and began the sacred rituals. He blessed the gathering with a long prayer, dropping handfuls of cedar needles on the coals and chanting. Clouds of pungent gray cedar smoke rose into the air.

The drums continued the slow and rhythmic tempo. Tokala Fire Eyes drew three whiffs of smoke into his lungs from the red stone pipe. And then blew them out; first breath at the Zenith; second breath on the ground, the third breath—Tokala Fire Eyes lifted his chin and blew the last breath up towards the Sun. He gathered the smoke with the eagle feather and walked around the circle, slowly waving the smoke towards the group; shaking the eagle feather fan in the direction of Yawns-a-Lot and at Kah-La, the other warriors and men and women. Everyone "pulled" the smoke toward their bodies and patted it over themselves and chanted. They thought of and prayed for and remembered their lost ancestors.

Tokala Fire Eyes held up a necklace made of lion's teeth, for all to see. He was proud of their youngest warrior. He smiled and continued chanting another long prayer as Opa Little Wing and Satinka Doe Foot and the others beat their drums louder.

The elders would have to decide what name to give this winter in their count of the years. They would also have to consider what to do about the white man's continuing theft and desecration of their lands. But tonight, "the people" would put on their best and beat the drums. Every dance would be a prayer. Every song would tell a story. They would exchange gifts and smoke the pipe of peace with new allies. While the festivities were overshadowed by "the peoples" continued loss—a celebration was being had to remember.

Tonight the air was filled with the fragrance of pinion smoke. The drums beat with an insistent cadence. The community would look to their future and Kah-La would finally claim his name: Buffalo-Stands-Firm.

Butterfly

I am but a shadow of my past; a reflection of those who bore my blood, hundreds of years ago. I am an image of those people, who have caused pain and suffering as well as those who have suffered mightily. My search for self has been long and premeditated, but prayerful. My steps were as awkward as a baby gazelle's, but as relentless as a badger, protecting its cub. The journey to the outside of my inner world has been filled with trepidation, betrayal, and forgiveness; as well as an abundance of love.

Protected by my higher being; the I am of who I AM,

I have examined the boundaries of my woman hood.

Thru chrysalis, I have become a butterfly.

Made in the USA
Monee, IL
15 November 2020